P9-DOH-538

Be THANKFUL

PEANUTS WISDOM TO CARRY YOU THROUGH

Running Press Kids
Hachette Book Group
1290 Avenue of the Americas, New York, NY 10104
www.runningpress.com/rpkids
@RP_Kids

Printed in China

First Edition: September 2013

Published by Running Press Kids, an imprint of Perseus Books, LLC,
a subsidiary of Hachette Book Group, Inc. The Running Press Kids
name and logo is a trademark of the Hachette Book Group.

The Hachette Speakers Bureau provides a wide range of authors for speaking events.
To find out more, go to www.hachettespeakersbureau.com or call (866) 376-6591.

The publisher is not responsible for websites (or their content)
that are not owned by the publisher.

Artwork created by Charles M. Schulz
For Charles M. Schulz Creative Associates: pencils by Vicki Scott,
inks by Paige Braddock, colors by Donna Almendrala
Print book cover and interior design by Frances J. Soo Ping Chow

Library of Congress Control Number: 2013940510

ISBN: 978-0-7624-5045-9 (hardcover)

1010

12 11 10 9 8 7 6 5 4 3

Be
Satisfied

PEANUTS

Be
THANKFUL

PEANUTS WISDOM TO CARRY YOU THROUGH

Based on the comic strip, PEANUTS,
by Charles M. Schulz

RUNNING PRESS

PHILADELPHIA

"Just remember, when you're over the hill, you begin to pick up speed."

—*Charles M. Schulz*

Linus: What do you mean, a good day?
It's raining . . . It's windy . . . It's cold!

Lucy: It's a good day to be crabby!

APPRECIATIVE

"In our family, the older we get, the cuter we get!"
—*Snoopy*

Be
LUCKY

Linus: So far, you've had a pretty successful life, haven't you? I wonder how you did it.

Snoopy: I was lucky. I got a first round bye.

Be
Considerate

"Don't say I never do anything for you. I just took your blanket out of the dryer."

—*Lucy*

POSITIVE

"Some people don't like the month of March . . .
I don't mind it at all. When the wind blows, you
can fly your ears!"

—*Snoopy*

Be
UPBEAT

Be

OPTIMISTIC

"I can't believe it. Our baseball season starts today, and we haven't lost yet. Of course, I haven't gotten out of bed yet, either."

—*Charlie Brown*

Be
Fulfilled

"You'll never convince me that there's more to life than chocolate chip cookies."

—*Snoopy*

Be
PLEASED

Charlie Brown: Dogs are really kind of peculiar. All they ever think about is eating. I call it a lack of depth.

Snoopy: I prefer to think of it as a singleness of purpose!

SURPRISED

"When it's cold, stay in your igloo and bake
chocolate chip cookies."

—*Snoopy*

Linus: Do you realize that you spend all your time complaining?

Lucy: Why shouldn't I complain? It's the only thing I'm really good at!

Be
MINDFUL

Charlie Brown: Airing out your blanket, Linus?

Linus: No, I hang it in the sun once a month as a gesture of appreciation for all it has done for me.

Be
ENTHUSIASTIC

Be
WARM

Be

Sentimental

"My pitcher's mound may be covered with snow, but the memories are still here."

—*Charlie Brown*

Be
CARING

Lucy: Well, thank you. You're a good brother.

Linus: Happiness is a compliment from your sister!

"I'm outrageously happy in my stupidity!"

—*Snoopy*

Be
Charitable

Lucy: It always feels good to give something to those Santas who stand on the corner.

Franklin: I agree.

Be

GENEROUS

"The gift of a flower is always a gift of love!"

—*Lucy*

Be

Friendly

OPEN

"When you live alone in the desert, you have to enjoy what you can. . . ."

—*Spike*

ACCEPTING

"I always have the vanilla on the bottom and the chocolate on top. You like to have the vanilla on top and the chocolate on the bottom? It takes all kinds to make the world!"

—*Snoopy*

OBSERVANT

"Let's just sit here for a while and enjoy the view."

—*Snoopy*

Be
JOYOUS

"Happiness is having your dog come home!"

—*Charlie Brown*

Be
PEACEFUL

Be
Selfless

Be
FESTIVE

Marcie: Does Monsieur Flying Ace know that next week is the birthday of the Red Baron?

Snoopy: She's right . . . I should send him a card. Something like, "Have a nice day."

Lucy: What do I have to be thankful for?

Linus: Well, for one thing, you have a little brother who loves you.

Be
EXPRESSIVE

Be
ADORED

"I never knew life could be so beautiful!"

—Peppermint Patty

Be
WISE

Charlie Brown: I have a new philosophy. "Life is like a golf course."

Snoopy: And "A sand trap runs through it."

Be Fortunate

Lucy: We are all capable of loving and
being loved.

Be
CHALLENGED

Be
HOPEFUL

Be **FREE!**